For Katie
and her Special Friends
SBB

To the Linn Creek ladies
with love and gratitude
RGK

Text by Roxie Kelley
Illustrations by Sherri Buck Baldwin
© Copyright 1999
All Rights Reserved
Made in the U.S.A.

10 9 8 7 6 5 4 3

Published by Lang Books,
A Division of R. A. Lang Card Company, Ltd.
514 Wells Street
Delafield, WI 53018

ISBN 0-7412-0284-0

To my very Special Friend:

Claudia

with love from:

Suzanne

Christmas 2000

Date

The most special friendships
are often formed when you're
busy thinking about something else.

With no walls up and your guard down,

You are charmed
by someone's unprotected presence.

J. Buck Baldwin © '91

One pleasant moment builds on another

Until you feel so connected that you
seem to be speaking
with one heart and one mind.

You find yourself smiling
when they smile,

J. Buck Baldwin © '92

You dream and scheme together;

Hope and cope together

Sharing the story of how
and why and when you
became friends
warms your heart.

And one day you realize
your life is brighter now.

You have a deeper understanding
of the words gratitude and growth,

And pleasure and peace...

It becomes clear how precious
this one life has become to you

And you know you
have been graced with
the gift of a
very Special friend.